Bushland Lullaby

For Ashton James and Imogen Grace — Sally Odgers

For Rachel and her rescued bush babies — Lisa Stewart

Scholastic Press
345 Pacific Highway Lindfield NSW 2070
An imprint of Scholastic Australia Pty Limited (ABN 11 000 614 577)
PO Box 579 Gosford NSW 2250
www.scholastic.com.au

Part of the Scholastic Group
Sydney • Auckland • New York • Toronto • London • Mexico City •
New Delhi • Hong Kong • Buenos Aires • Puerto Rico

First published by Scholastic Australia in 2012.
Text copyright © Sally Odgers, 2012.
Illustrations copyright © Lisa Stewart, 2012.

National Library of Australia Cataloguing-in-Publication entry
Author: Odgers, Sally Farrell, 1957-
Title: Bushland lullaby / Sally Odgers ; Lisa Stewart, illustrator.
ISBN: 978 1 74283 177 0 (hbk.)
      978 1 74283 178 7 (pbk.)
Target Audience: For pre-school age.
Subjects: Animals–Australia–Juvenile fiction.
         Lullabies, English–Australia.
Other Authors/Contributors: Stewart, Lisa, 1969- .
Dewey Number: A823.3

Typeset in Wilke, featuring Allura.
Illustrations created using watercolour, gouache, collage, rice papers and pencil.

Printed in Malaysia by Tien Wah Press.
Scholastic Australia's policy, in association with Tien Wah Press, is to use papers that are renewable and made efficiently
from wood grown in sustainable forests, so as to minimise its environmental footprint.

10 9 8 7 6 5 4 3 2   13 14 15 16 / 1

SALLY ODGERS   LISA STEWART

Bushland Lullaby

A Scholastic Press book from Scholastic Australia

In the sunlit gully, green and wide
Where secret nooks are fine to hide
In a soft and grassy snuggly nest
Little *bandicoot* comes to rest.

Snug in the hollow of an old gum tree

When the morning light is blithe to see

Asleep in a gently snoozing ball
Little *possum's* soft and small.

In a merry creek where the currents run
Where eddies dance with winking sun
Curled in a burrow so safe and deep
Little *platypus* lies asleep.

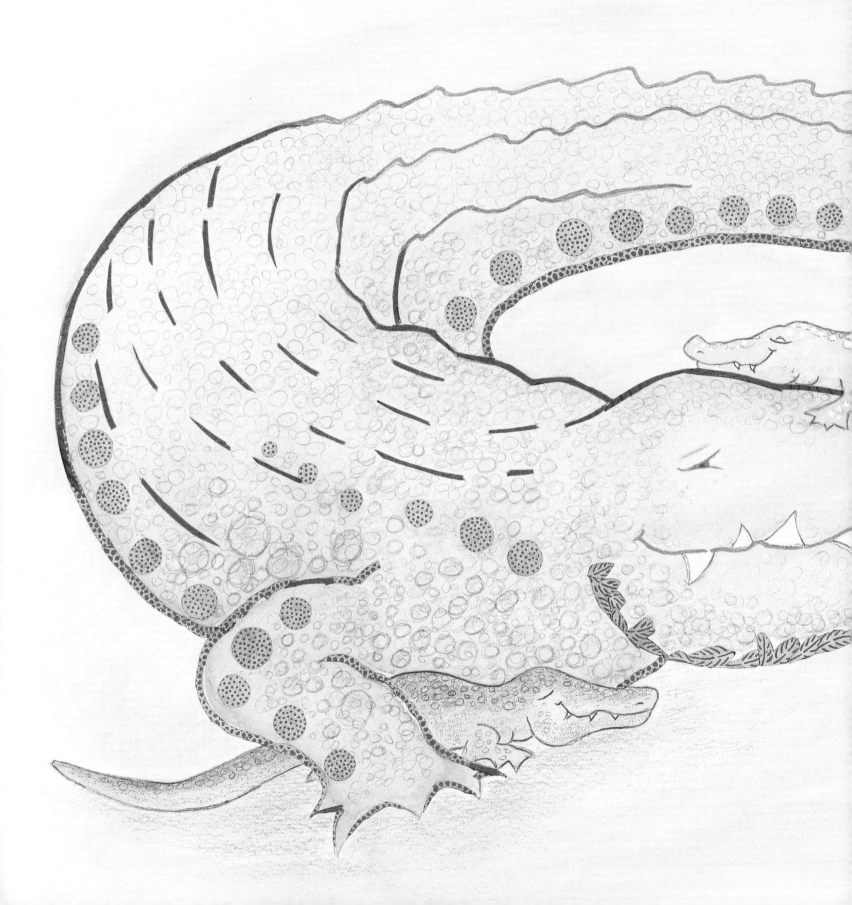

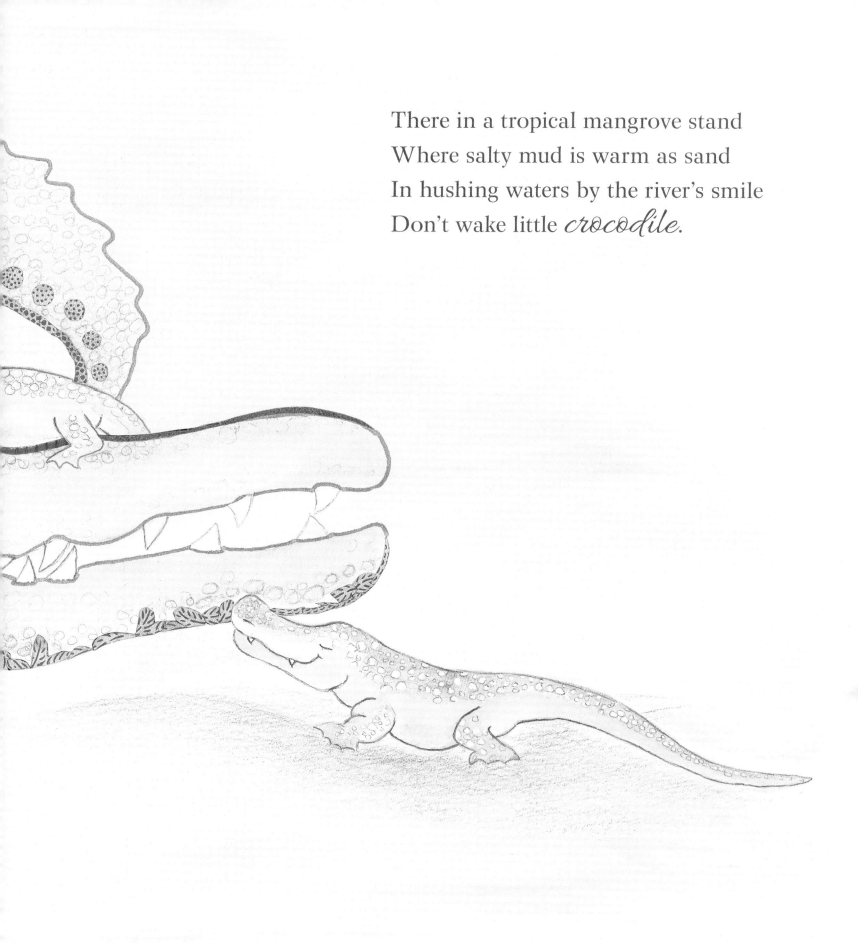

There in a tropical mangrove stand
Where salty mud is warm as sand
In hushing waters by the river's smile
Don't wake little *crocodile*.

On the scribbly trunk of a leaning tree
So still, so quiet, he's hard to see

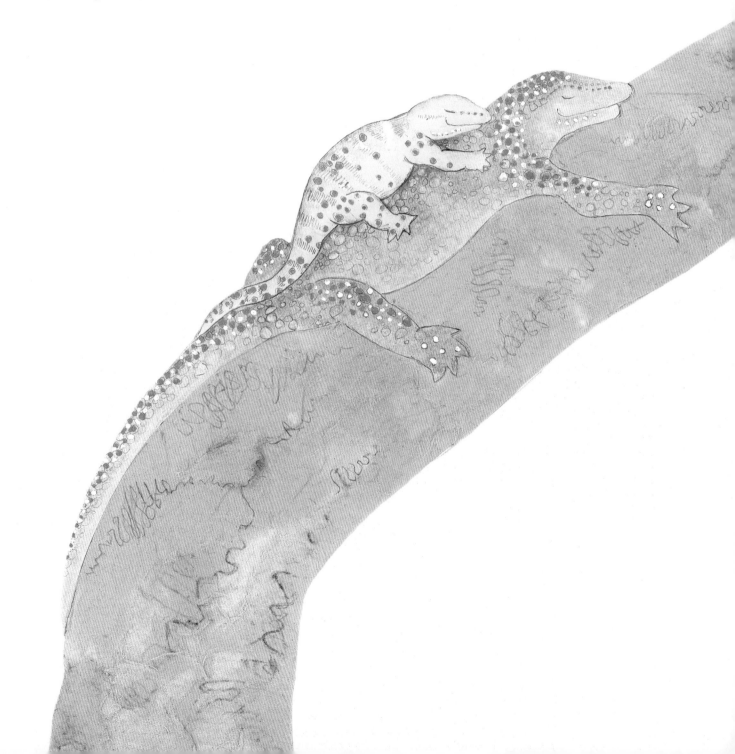

In the place he thinks is bushland's best
Little *goanna* clings to rest.

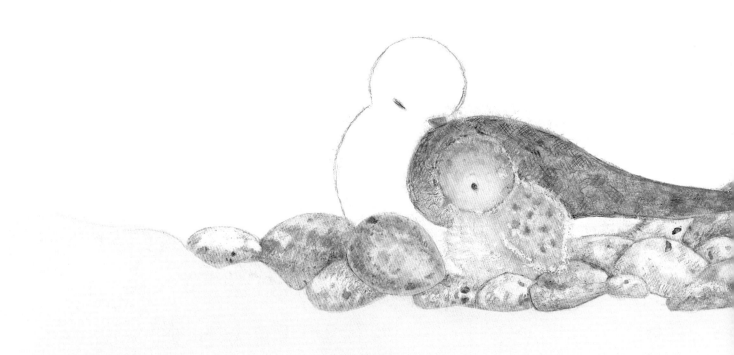

There's a lonely island in the sea
Where breakers sing when the wind blows free
In a pebbled nest out of water's reach
Little *seagull*'s on the beach.

On a shivering island clad with snow
Where the ocean kisses icy floes
In a stony nest with her mother close
Little *penguin* may safely doze.

In the wattle grove, under dappled skies
When the drifting clouds fly soft and high
Through the afternoon of restful hours
Little *wallaby* comes to drowse.

Down in the bush where the gum trees thrive
Where the lazy breeze brings scents alive
In the lofty fork of an ancient tree
Little *koala* goes to sleep.

Burrowed into an earthy mound
In the summer day when the sun bakes down
In a twisty tunnel and cosy bed
Little *wombat* rests his head.

Hung like fruit in a tropical park
In bundles strangely plump and dark
When the sunset's pink and the cricket zings
Little *fruit bat's* wrapped in wings.